Camdean

KU-067-802

Item no.   00384

David Alderton
Studio Boni/Galante
Paola Holguín

adybird

CONTENTS

SEAS AND OCEANS

Nearly three-quarters of the Earth's surface is covered by oceans. These were first formed millions of years ago, as volcanoes produced steam, which cooled and became water. The salty taste of the sea comes from some of the **minerals**, especially sodium, which have dissolved into the water from the land.

What is a sea?
The world's oceans are divided into seven smaller areas, called seas. Some inland lakes are also known as seas, especially if they are very large and contain salty water.

CURRENTS, WAVES AND TIDES

The movement of water in the world's oceans is caused by currents. These follow set patterns, triggered by winds. Currents circulate the water, and help to even out the temperature in the entire ocean. Cold water from the **Poles** is forced towards the **Equator**, and so becomes warmer as a result. Other currents from the Equator then move water back towards the Poles.

Currents also occur close to land. Here they can be very dangerous, sweeping swimmers unexpectedly away from the shore.

The fastest current in the world is the Agulhas Current which flows along the west coast of Africa. It moves at a speed of about eight kilometres per hour.

Waves

Wind blowing on the surface of the sea causes **waves**. As the wind speed increases, so white tops appear on waves. The stronger the wind, the bigger the waves. When a wave hits a beach, it finally breaks up, and water drains back into the sea.

Tides

The way in which the sea moves up-and-down the beach each day depends on the **tides**. You can often spot the high tide mark, especially after a storm. This is where seaweed and other debris from the sea is left in a rough line, high up on the beach.

The daily effect of the orbit of the Moon around the Earth.

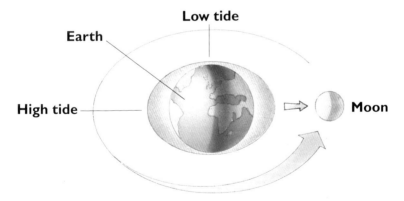

Low tide

Earth

High tide

Moon

Tides are the result of the daily pull of the Moon's **gravity** on the sea. Tide levels vary each day and in different parts of the world. When the Moon and Sun are aligned with the Earth, the gravitational pull becomes stronger, which causes higher tides. This happens about once every two weeks. At other times, neap tides occur. There is then less difference between high and low tides. The biggest tides occur in eastern Canada.

SAVING THE SEAS

Pollution is a major threat to sea life. Steps are being taken to protect our marine environment. More than 300 areas round the world are now protected, and many governments have introduced laws that deter companies from polluting the seas.

Danger from sewage
Releasing raw **sewage** into the sea is dangerous because harmful bacteria can survive in water.

Hazards from ships
Oil spillages from damaged tankers kill large numbers of sea birds and other marine life.

Waste
Rubbish thrown from ships can be very dangerous to wildlife.

Recently, overfishing has led to a decline in the numbers of popular food fish, such as tuna and shark. Controls are now being imposed to prevent fish from becoming **endangered**. Another environmental concern is the dumping of barrels of **toxic waste** into the sea. Toxic waste could eventually leak out of the barrels into the sea.

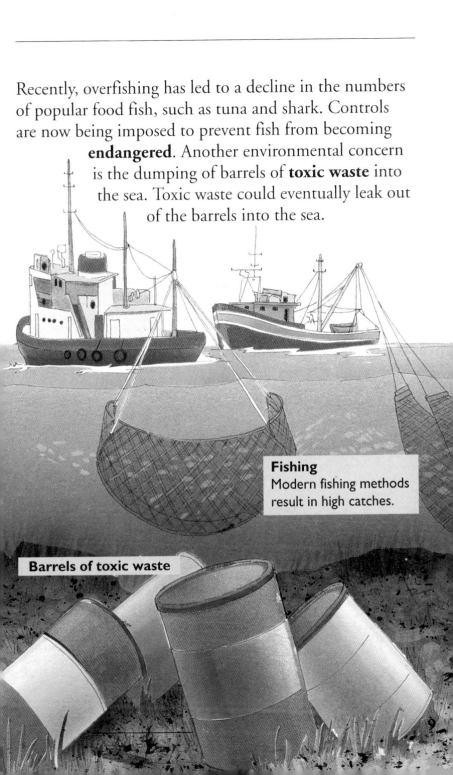

Fishing
Modern fishing methods result in high catches.

Barrels of toxic waste

ALONG THE SEASHORE

A seashore can be pebbly or sandy. Beach sand is made up from rocks and seashells, which have been broken up by the sea into very fine particles. The origins of the sand affect its colour. Coral will give sand a whitish appearance, while yellow sand contains quartz, and black sand has either coal or volcanic rock in it.

In some areas, cliffs may make it impossible to reach the seashore. Waves crash directly against the cliff face, wearing it away and carving out caves and arches.

Birds
At low tide, wading birds wander through **rock pools**.

Curlews
These birds use their long, pointed beaks to probe through sand in search of worms.

Seashore life

Animals that live along the seashore and in rock pools have to cope with the daily rise and fall of tides. Limpets cling tightly to the rocks so that they are not swept out to sea. Seaweeds have root-like anchors to hold on to rocks. Seaweeds are also coated in slime to stop them drying up when the tide is out.

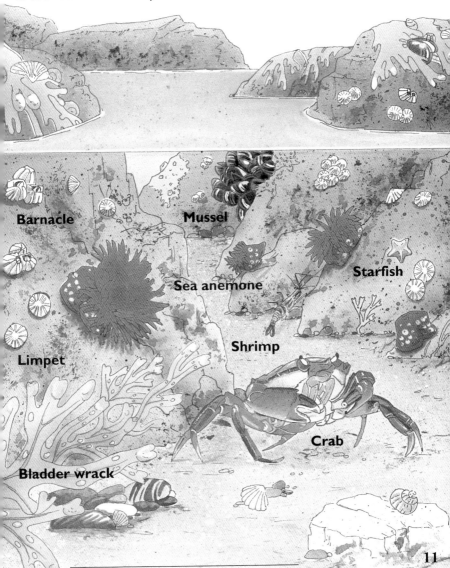

Barnacle

Mussel

Sea anemone

Starfish

Shrimp

Limpet

Crab

Bladder wrack

UNDERSEA LANDSCAPES

Around the edges of the land the seabed slopes before
dropping down quite steeply into water, which may be
four kilometres deep. The bottom of the sea is just as
varied as dry land. Deep valleys, high mountain ranges,
volcanoes and great plains stretch over this vast,
submerged area of our planet.

Deep sea trenches

There are deep troughs in the
seabed, called **trenches**. The
Marianas Trench in the Pacific
Ocean is over eleven kilometres
deep. This is the deepest point in
all the oceans.

DEEP SEA MOUNTAINS

The longest mountain range in the world is the Mid-Atlantic Ridge, which lies mainly under the sea.

Abyssal plains

Deep below the surface of the sea are flat areas called **abyssal plains**. These plains make up about half the ocean floor.

Seamounts

Isolated underwater mountains rise up from the ocean floor. One of the biggest **seamounts** is the Great Meteor Seamount in the Atlantic Ocean.

13

OCEAN FISH

Fish can be found throughout the world's oceans. Few creatures are as adaptable as fish. In the Antarctic Ocean, for example, ice fish have developed special chemicals in their blood to help them stay warm.

COD
*Cod live in **shoals** close to the ocean surface. When breeding, cod scatter their eggs in the sea.*

Flying fish
These swim near the surface and leap out of the water if in danger.

Sharks
These are the most feared fish in the sea. But not all sharks are dangerous. Nor are they all large.

FLATFISH
*When they first hatch, **flatfish** are shaped like normal fish. But as a flatfish grows older, one of its eyes gradually moves round to the upper side of its body. It then starts to swim using the fins around the edge of its body.*

Deep below the surface of the sea, the water is inky black and icy cold. Water is heavy and the weight of water creates enormous pressure – enough to crush a person. Despite such conditions, many weird and wonderful creatures live in the deepest, darkest parts of our seas.

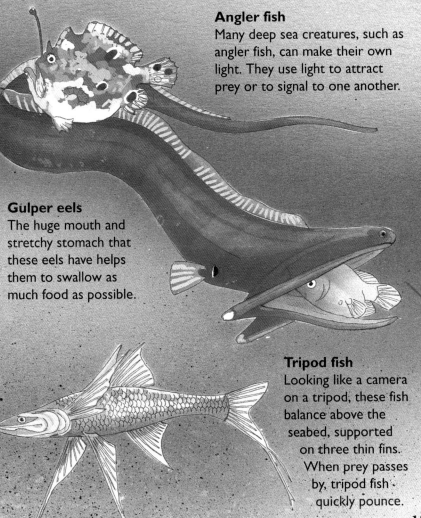

Angler fish
Many deep sea creatures, such as angler fish, can make their own light. They use light to attract prey or to signal to one another.

Gulper eels
The huge mouth and stretchy stomach that these eels have helps them to swallow as much food as possible.

Tripod fish
Looking like a camera on a tripod, these fish balance above the seabed, supported on three thin fins. When prey passes by, tripod fish quickly pounce.

MARINE REPTILES

Marine reptiles live mainly in the tropical seas, where the water is warm. This allows them to maintain their body temperatures, whereas in colder waters they would become less active. There are fewer than sixty species of marine reptile alive today, but the world's oceans used to be home to many more different types, which are now known only as **fossils**.

Leatherback turtle
The leatherback turtle is the largest of the world's seven varieties of sea turtle. This turtle swims throughout the world's oceans.

Sea snake
There are about fifty different types of sea snake. They can be brightly coloured, and they are all highly poisonous. Sea snakes feed mainly on fish.

SEA CROCODILE
Some crocodiles can live in both fresh and salty water. Crocodiles of the Indian and Pacific Oceans are the biggest and most dangerous types of crocodile. At sea, crocodiles often drift with the currents.

SEA BIRDS

Many birds live close to the coast, coming inland when the weather is bad. Others use cliff faces as secure nesting sites, where they breed in huge colonies. A few birds, such as albatrosses, spend long periods gliding over the oceans, far away from land. They drop down to scoop up fish from the sea.

Frigate bird
This 'pirate of the skies' steals its food from other sea birds. It forces them to drop their catch and then grabs the food before it falls into the sea.

Pelican
The huge, expandable pouch under a pelican's beak acts like a fishing net. A pelican catches fish by trawling with its mouth open under the water. It then sieves the water, so it can swallow its catch.

Oystercatcher
This is one of a group of wading birds, which lives along the shoreline. The oystercatcher uses its blunt beak like a chisel to knock shellfish off the rocks.

PREHISTORIC SEA CREATURES

The first animals with backbones which evolved in the seas were fish. Their fossils have been traced back nearly 500 million years. Early fish were very different in appearance from those which live in the oceans today, but they did have gills. This meant that they could obtain oxygen from the water without coming up to the surface to breathe air.

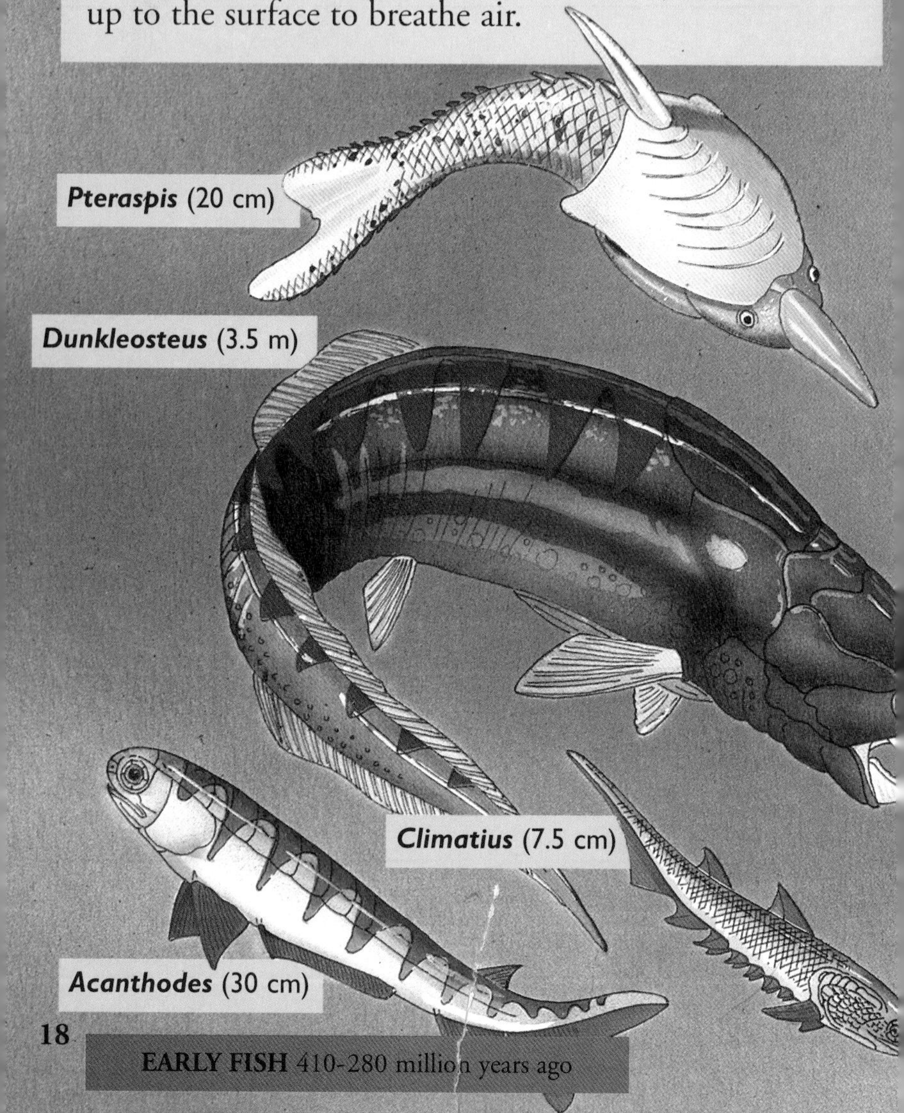

Pteraspis (20 cm)

Dunkleosteus (3.5 m)

Climatius (7.5 cm)

Acanthodes (30 cm)

EARLY FISH 410-280 million years ago

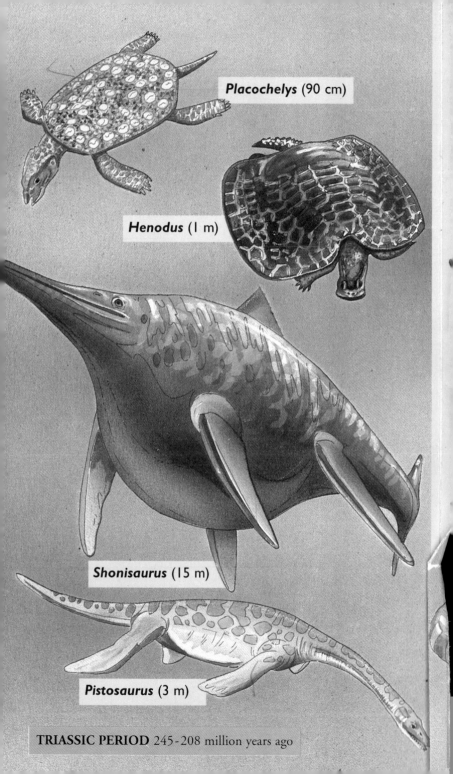

Placochelys (90 cm)

Henodus (1 m)

Shonisaurus (15 m)

Pistosaurus (3 m)

TRIASSIC PERIOD 245-208 million years ago

Herring

Mackerel

Cod

Sardine

Blue shark

THE DISCOVERY OF THE COELACANTH

In 1938, a fishing boat caught a strange fish which the crewmen did not recognise. Back in port, they asked an expert from the local museum to identify the fish for them. It turned out to be a coelacanth. Previously, these fish had only been known as fossils and they were thought to have been extinct for more than sixty million years. The coelacanth is now a protected fish.

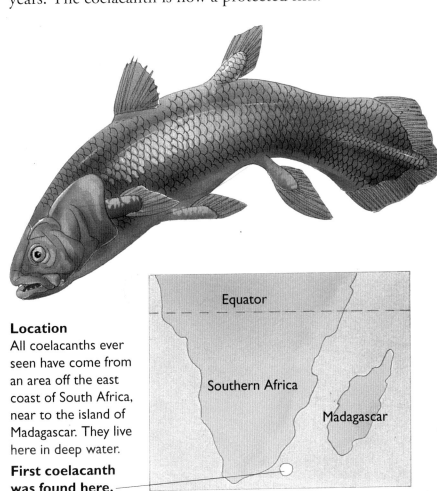

Location
All coelacanths ever seen have come from an area off the east coast of South Africa, near to the island of Madagascar. They live here in deep water.

First coelacanth was found here.

Equator

Southern Africa

Madagascar

SEA MAMMALS

All sea mammals are excellent swimmers. They have flippers, which help them to swim. Some sea mammals, such as whales and dolphins, spend their whole lives in the water and others, such as seals and walruses, divide their time between land and sea.

Sea otter

This sea mammal cleverly winds strands of seaweed around itself to stop it drifting away with the tide while it is sleeping. Sea otters place their front paws over their eyes when asleep.

Sea lion

Sea lions can swim faster than all other seals. They may reach a speed of 40 kilometres per hour for short distances.

Whale

All mammals need air to breathe. Whales can hold their breath for several hours underwater, but sooner or later, they have to come up for air.

DANGER AND ESCAPING DANGER

Octopus
If threatened, an octopus squirts a cloud of dark 'ink' to confuse its predator.

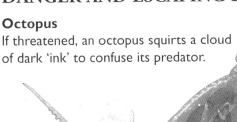

Sea cucumber
To escape from an attacker, the sea cucumber shoots out strings of sticky, spaghetti-like threads. The attacker is then too busy trying to disentangle itself to bother with the sea cucumber.

Stonefish
The stonefish is perfectly **camouflaged**. It looks just like a harmless stone on the seabed, but it is covered with deadly poisonous spines. The sting of this fish can kill people.

LIFE ON A CORAL REEF

Coral reefs grow in warm, shallow water in tropical seas. The coral is made up of millions of tiny sea creatures called coral **polyps**. The polyps build stony cases around their soft bodies for protection. When they die, the hard cases remain and gradually build up into a reef. A third of all fish live amongst the world's coral reefs.

Parrot fish

Pipe fish

Clown fish

Angelfish

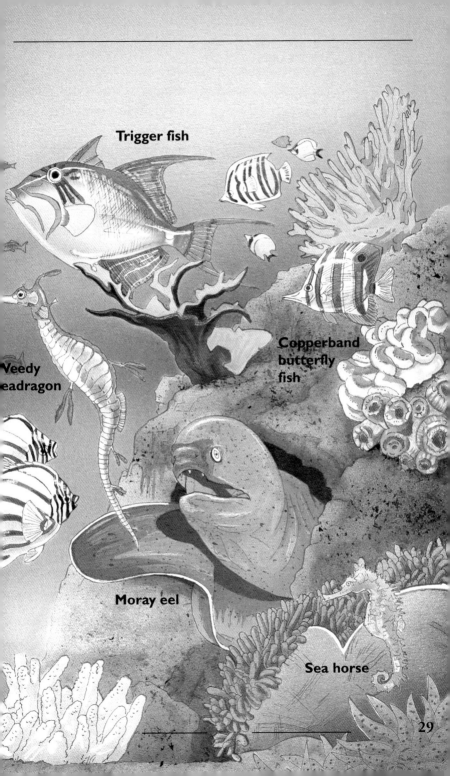

Trigger fish

Copperband
butterfly
fish

Veedy
eadragon

Moray eel

Sea horse

SEA GIANTS AND DWARFS

Thousands of different kinds of animals and plants live in the sea. They come in a huge variety of shapes and sizes, from the gigantic blue whale to tiny plants that are smaller than pinheads.

Blue whale

The blue whale is the largest animal in the world. It is a mammal that lives in the sea.

Atlantic giant squid

This squid has the largest eyes of any known animal. The largest squid ever known was washed ashore in Newfoundland in 1878. Its tentacles were eleven metres in length.

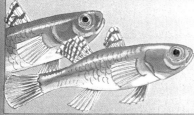

DWARF GOBY

The smallest fish in the sea is the tiny dwarf goby, which lives in the Indian Ocean. Fully grown, it is less than one centimetre in length.

Whale shark

The biggest fish in the sea, the whale shark, grows up to at least twelve metres in length, and weighs over fifteen tonnes. It feeds mainly on **phytoplankton** and is not dangerous.

Pacific giant kelp

A single strand of this seaweed can measure over 60 metres in length, which makes it the biggest sea plant. It also grows very fast.

PHYTOPLANKTON

The smallest sea plants are phytoplankton. They drift on the surface, providing food for many sea animals, but they can only be seen under a microscope.

EXPLORING THE SEA

For thousands of years, people have sailed the seas. Their boats ranged in style from simple dug-out canoes to huge oil tankers. The earliest ocean journeys were voyages of exploration. Sailors relied on the Sun, Moon and stars to help **navigate**. Later, merchants searched for trade routes around the world.

A Polynesian raft

The Polynesian people built canoes from hollowed out tree trunks. Two canoes could be fixed together to make a raft. The Polynesian sailors used both sails and paddles to propel the boat. They strung seashells onto sticks, to make maps of the many islands in the South Pacific Ocean.

Exploring the oceans

Ferdinand Magellan left Spain with five ships and 260 men in 1519, in search of a westerly route to the Spice Islands, west of Papua New Guinea. Although the expedition eventually succeeded, Magellan was killed, and only one of the ships and eighteen men survived. It was the first round the world voyage.

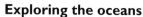

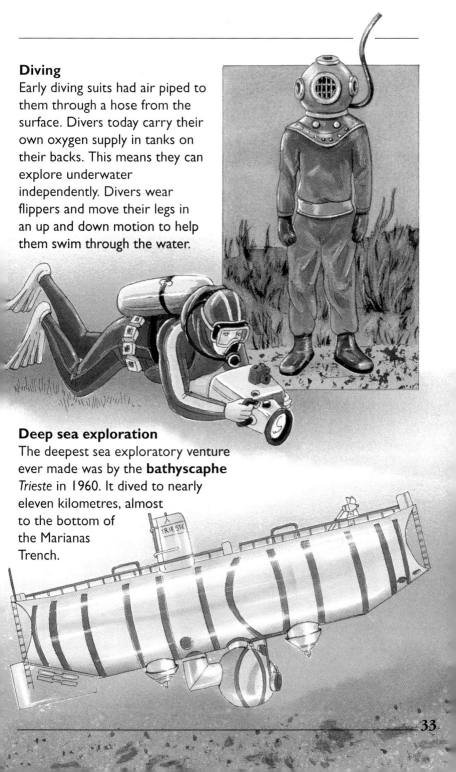

Diving

Early diving suits had air piped to them through a hose from the surface. Divers today carry their own oxygen supply in tanks on their backs. This means they can explore underwater independently. Divers wear flippers and move their legs in an up and down motion to help them swim through the water.

Deep sea exploration

The deepest sea exploratory venture ever made was by the **bathyscaphe** *Trieste* in 1960. It dived to nearly eleven kilometres, almost to the bottom of the Marianas Trench.

TREASURES OF THE SEA

The sea is a vast treasure trove of useful and valuable things. Scientists analyse seabed rocks in search of oil or gas. Wells are drilled into the seabed and oil or gas is pumped up. Fish and other sea creatures are caught as food, and even seaweed is useful. It may be eaten, or used as a fertilizer.

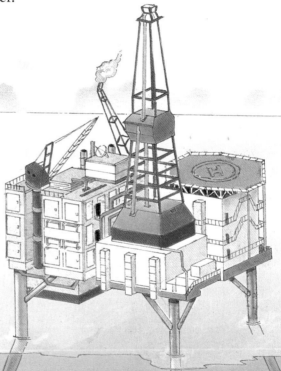

An oil rig
Drilling for oil and gas in the sea is expensive and often dangerous. People live and work on the oil rig, usually for two weeks at a time. They are flown on and off the rig by helicopter.

TREASURE IN A SHELL
A pearl is formed if an oyster or clam shell has a speck of sand inside its shell. The oyster covers the speck with layers of a chemical called calcium carbonate. This builds up into a pearl.

Finding treasure

Underwater archaeologists study historical records of ships which sank. Archaeologists plan their search carefully on land, trying to locate where the ship was lost. Only then does diving start.

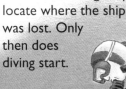

Treasure, ranging from gold bars and jewellery to ancient cargoes of porcelain, still lies undiscovered in sunken shipwrecks all over the world's seabeds.

Underwater exploration

In deep water, submersible craft can be used to find wrecks, photograph them and even help to retrieve ancient artefacts.

AMAZING SEA FACTS

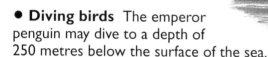

- **Deepest living fish**
Brotulid fish have been found
in the Puerto Rico Trench,
8,366 metres below the
surface of the Atlantic Ocean.

- **Diving birds** The emperor
penguin may dive to a depth of
250 metres below the surface of the sea.

- **Largest sea** The South China Sea, off the coast of Asia, is
the largest sea in the world. It contains many small islands and
has valuable stores of both gas and oil under its seabed.

- **Clearest water** It is possible to see an object which is
30 centimetres across, down to a depth of 80 metres below
the surface, in the Weddell Sea, close to Antarctica.

- **Greatest number of eggs** The female ocean sunfish may
lay as many as 30 million eggs at one time.

- **Sea bird droppings** Huge pillars of bird droppings,
some more than 90 metres tall, have built up over thousands of
years from colonies of sea birds nesting on islands off the coast
of Peru, South America. In the 1800s,
many columns were destroyed when it
was realised they could be sold as a
fertilizer, called guano.

- **Largest ocean** The Pacific is the
largest ocean in the world. Excluding
the seas surrounding it, the Pacific
represents nearly 50 per cent of
the world's oceans.

- **Gold mine** More than 60,000 tonnes
of gold have been found in the sea. All
of the chemical elements exist in the
world's oceans.

GLOSSARY

Abyssal plain A flat area occurring below the surface of the sea, sometimes in the deepest part of the oceans.

Bathyscaphe An underwater craft, used for exploring the deepest parts of the sea.

Camouflage The way in which a creature hides itself, using its body shape or colour to blend into the background.

Endangered When a species is in danger of dying out altogether and disappearing from the Earth.

Equator An imaginary line that runs round the middle of the Earth.

Flatfish A fish such as a plaice or a flounder, which has a flattened body shape.

Fossil The remains or impression of an animal or plant that have been preserved in the Earth.

Gravity The force that pulls the sea towards the Moon, creating tides.

Mineral A chemical that is present on land and may dissolve in water.

Navigate To direct or steer the course of a ship on a journey.

Phytoplankton Microscopic plants present in the oceans, which are a vital source of food for many sea creatures.

Poles The most northern and southerly parts of the Earth.

Pollution Damaging the environment with chemicals and waste materials.

Polyps Minute creatures whose remains gradually build up into a coral reef.

Rock pool The rocky area that still contains water when the tide goes out.

Seamount An underwater mountain that can rise from the seabed to a height of 4,000 metres.

Sewage Waste material.

Shoal A group of the same fish swimming together.

Tide The regular, daily movement of the sea up and down the beach.

Toxic waste Poisonous waste material.

Trench Crack in the seabed, which forms the deepest part of the oceans.

Wave The surface movement of the sea, caused by winds.

INDEX *(Entries in **bold** refer to an illustration)*